Frightful's Daughter

by JEAN CRAIGHEAD GEORGE

illustrated by DANIEL SAN SOUCI

DUTTON CHILDREN'S BOOKS – NEW YORK

Text copyright © 2002 by Jean Craighead George
Illustrations copyright © 2002 by Daniel San Souci

CIP Data is available.

Published in the United States 2002 by Dutton Children's Books,
a division of Penguin Putnam Books for Young Readers
345 Hudson Street, New York, New York 10014
www.penguinputnam.com

Designed by Gloria Cheng

Printed in Hong Kong
First Edition
ISBN 0-525-46907-9
1 3 5 7 9 10 8 6 4 2

To the memory of my brother
Frank C. Craighead Jr., peregrine lover

J.C.G.

For Lucia, who gave me the opportunity
to illustrate the work of this beloved
and renowned author

D.S.S.

OKSI broke out of her rosy cream-colored egg. The wet down on her head stood up straight. Her bulging eyes were sealed shut. Her beak was pale blue and large. Oksi was an eyas, a rare and precious peregrine falcon chick. She was the daughter of Frightful, a falcon of legend in the Catskill Mountains.

From the day she hatched, Oksi did things her own way. She ate when she should have been sleeping. She stood up when she should have sat. When she was eight days old, her big black eyes opened wide and she could see. She hobbled to the edge of the falcon aerie, her home on a girder of a high bridge.

Looking out, she saw the river valley and a quiet mountain.

She saw her mother, Frightful, in the sky above her.

"Rehk, rehk, rehk! Danger!" Frightful screamed to her three little eyases. Her wing feathers rustled like fans as she looped and dove. "Rehk, rehk, rehk, rehk! Danger!"

Oksi and her brothers were too young to fly. They could only freeze and remain still. They pulled in their necks and flattened their feathers. On their nest of sticks, they seemed to be riverside stones. All but Oksi, who did things her own way.

She backed into the shadow of a bridge support.

The danger was a man. He had climbed the bridge to the aerie. He grabbed Oksi's brothers, one in each hand. They stabbed at him with their talons.

"You're strong and fat," the falcon thief said. "You'll bring a good price on the illegal market." Knowing that peregrine falcons are protected by law, he glanced around to see if a cop was watching him, then quickly stuffed the eyases into a leather sack.

He started down the truss. Frightful struck him in a steep dive from far up above the bridge. He teetered under the powerful blow, rubbed his head, then hurriedly climbed on down to the roadway. Frightful did not give up. She chased after him. She hit his shoulder with her talons as he got into his truck. She dove at the truck as she followed it down the road.

Oksi stayed in the shadows of the girder.

Hours passed. Everything in the valley was quiet. She waited for Frightful to come back.

"Kochee, kochee! I'm here!" Oksi called to her mother, but Frightful did not return. She thought all her babies had been stolen. She could not count.

"Kochee!" Oksi called, louder and louder.

Sam Gribley heard the call. He lived in a giant tree on the top of a beautiful mountain nearby. He lived there because he loved the forest and the wild birds and mammals.

Sam knew all about Frightful and her family. She was his falcon. One spring, when she was a baby, he had taken her from her nest. He had named her Frightful and trained her to hunt game with him. He turned her free when he learned to hunt with a slingshot. But she was still part of his life. This spring he had watched her and her strong mate incubate and hatch three lively babies.

And he happened to be watching when the thief climbed the bridge, stole the eyases, and drove away. Enraged, he had bolted down the mountain to stop him but arrived too late. The thief was gone.

Then Oksi called again, "KOCHEE, KOCHEE! I'm here!"

Sam climbed swiftly to her.

"Don't be afraid," he whispered. "I'm a friend of your mother's." He picked her up gently. "The thief will probably be back for you. I'm taking you home."

Sam carried Oksi up the mountain to his home in the giant hemlock tree. He fed her lots of food, then lifted her into a wooden box just outside. He had made it for Frightful, hoping she would nest in it. Of course, she had not. She was a peregrine falcon, a bird of open waterways and broad valleys. She had picked a place more suited to her spirit, on a girder of the high bridge over the river. Frightful was not a bird of the forest.

"This is your new home," Sam said to Oksi. "And I am your new mother. Stay in the box, or the owl who lives in that oak will get you."

But Oksi did things her own way.

She hopped out on the perch Sam had nailed to the front of the box and stood in plain view of the owl. She screamed, "KOCHEE, KOCHEE! I'm here! I'm here!"

This time Frightful, her real mother, heard her. She bombed down from the sky and lit beside Oksi. The frightened owl flew off.

Oksi greeted Frightful with an open beak.

Sam cheered and whistled "Hello" to Frightful. She called back, as she had done when they had hunted together.

"You haven't forgotten me," he called, then added, "I know you don't like a nest in the forest, but I'll make it up to you. Stay and take care of Oksi, and I'll help you hunt for her food."

But to Frightful his offer didn't matter. Her nest was where Oksi was. She walked into the box and opened her wings, and her eyas ran under them.

With lots of good food provided by Sam and Frightful, Oksi grew quickly. Feathers replaced her baby down. Her large eyes became keen-sighted. Her pale crown and back changed to gray-brown. Her flight feathers grew long and straight.

One day when Oksi was five weeks old, she flapped her wings. They lifted her off her feet. She dropped back down and flapped them again. She went up in the air and down.

"Rehk, rehk, rehk! Don't fly!" Frightful warned. The shafts of Oksi's flight feathers were still soft. They needed to harden.

"Rehk! Rehk! Don't fly!"

But Oksi did things her own way. She lifted her wings, pulled them down, then up, down—and was flying.

Oksi flapped over Sam's ancient hemlock tree and soared down the mountain. Frightful soared right behind her.

Sadly, Sam watched them go. Nesting time was over. The falcons would not be back. They would roost in the big trees along the river and hunt the waterfowl there. That was their world, not here in the forest. But Sam put some food out for Oksi just in case she had trouble learning to hunt. If she did, she would come back to her nest for food.

No sooner had Oksi flown from the nest box than a powerful goshawk spotted her. Oksi was flapping awkwardly below him. He knew her talons were dangerous, but not her back. He stooped to kill.

Oksi did things her own way. She saw him coming, turned upside down, and struck him with her talons. The goshawk sped off.

For the next month Frightful and Sam fed Oksi when she could not catch food. She was learning that hunting was not easy. Her prey were clever. But so was Oksi.

One day after she had missed three ducks, Oksi saw a man set a live trap. He was a licensed falconer who had permission to catch this wonderful bird and train her to hunt for him. He baited the trap with a live pigeon.

Oksi circled the tasty bird in the trap. But she was wary. She knew no pigeon would sit in a place like that.

Oksi did things her own way. She flew to the falconer's nearby pigeon cote, where she knew pigeons would be. She snapped up a nice, fat bird from the roof. There were many more pigeons for the taking.

For the rest of the summer, Oksi hunted the valley on her own in her own way. She returned often and feasted on the falconer's pigeons and on the wild geese that summered in the river bottomlands. When she failed to catch anything, she found the food that Sam put out. Those nights she slept in his hemlock tree.

The days grew shorter and colder, telling the migrant birds that it was time to go south. Frightful felt the urge of the changing seasons and circled Sam's mountain. She called to Oksi. It was time to migrate to South America for the winter. With Chup, her mate, they would go as a family.

Oksi heard the call. She saw Frightful face south, pump her wings, and take off with single-minded purpose. But Oksi did things her own way. She did not follow.

Oksi flew back to the valley. She was a spectacular flier now.

She rode the spirals of heat waves up into the October sky. She rolled in loops as she chased across November mountains.

One cold morning, she could not find food. The geese and ducks, the robins and warblers, had all flown south. This was a problem. Falcons must eat every day or they become too weak to hunt. Four days without food and they die.

On the second day without food, Oksi flew to the pigeon cote. It was sealed tight for the winter. Oksi sat on the roof. The wind blew. Snow swirled. The valley was white and still.

On the third day without food, Oksi was weak.

She worked her way back tree by tree to the nest box where Sam put out food. Not one morsel was there. She called out weakly, "Rehk, rehk, rehk." Sam burst out of his tree home.

"Oksi!" he shouted in astonishment. "What are you doing here? You should be in South America." He saw she was thin and went right to his tree pantry. He came back with part of a frozen duck and held it up.

Oksi was so hungry she flew to his hand. Sam carried her inside his warm tree home, where she tore the meat into small edible pieces. Then he put her on the foot of the bed.

"It's too late now for you to go south," he told her. "Your food has all flown away." Then he smiled. "You'll just have to stay here with me this winter and be my hunting partner like your mother was." He looked into her large black eyes.

"This was a good day for the two of us, Oksi," he said. He stroked her breast with a feather to relax her, the first step in her training.

All winter Sam and Oksi hunted together. They grew plump on pheasant and rabbit.

They watched the stars at night, and the squirrels by day. They talked to each other in soft peregrine whistles.

Then it was March. On a windy day Oksi spiraled into the sky and disappeared. Sam called and called, but she did not come back. And he knew she would not. Oksi was a peregrine falcon. The open skies and river courses, the vast seacoasts and high alpine tundras, were hers, not the forest.

Sam sighed and went fishing in his pond.

Many mornings later, when Sam was making acorn pancakes, he heard Oksi call. He looked up as she landed on the nest box. Her wings and back were a rich dark blue. Her head was jet black, her breast shone white. She was beautiful. It was springtime.

Speeding right behind her came Falco, a male peregrine falcon. He alighted on the perch, bowed to Oksi, and gave her a stick. She took it into the nest box and laid it down with great care. The first furniture for their home was in place.

Sam whistled in astonishment. "There are going to be baby peregrine falcons in a *forest!*"

Oksi did things her own way.